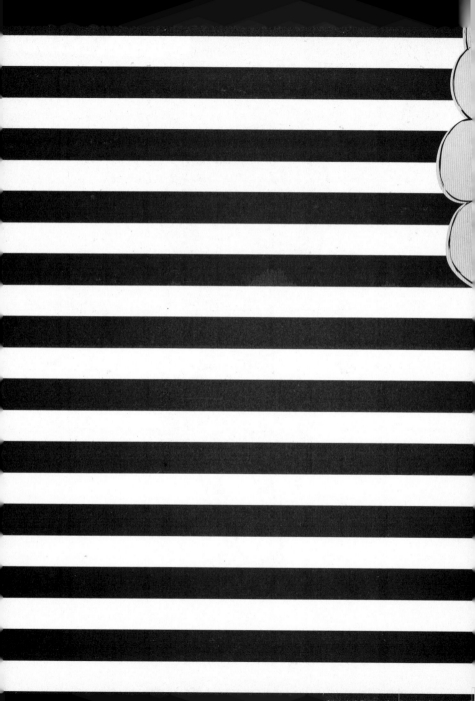

HEIDI HECKELBECK

in Disguise

By Wanda Coven

Illustrated by Priscilla Burris

LITTLE SIMON

New York London Toronto Sydney New Delhi

LITTLE SIMON
An imprint of Simon & Schuster Children's Publishing Division
1230 Avenue of the Americas, New York, New York 10020
Copyright © 2012 by Simon & Schuster, Inc.
All rights reserved, including the right of reproduction in whole or in part in any form.
LITTLE SIMON is a registered trademark of Simon & Schuster, Inc., and associated colophon is a trademark of Simon & Schuster, Inc.
For information about special discounts for bulk purchases, please contact Simon & Schuster Special Sales at 1-866-506-1949 or business@simonandschuster.com.
The Simon & Schuster Speakers Bureau can bring authors to your live event. For more information or to book an event contact the Simon & Schuster Speakers Bureau at 1-866-248-3049 or visit our website at www.simonspeakers.com.
Manufactured in the United States of America 0612 FFG
First Edition 10 9 8 7 6 5 4 3 2 1
Library of Congress Cataloging-in-Publication Data
Coven, Wanda.
Heidi Heckelbeck in disguise / by Wanda Coven ; illustrated by Priscilla Burris.
— 1st ed.
p. cm.
Summary: Witch Heidi is angry when mean Melanie Maplethorpe dresses as a witch for Halloween, but when she decides to retaliate, she almost loses all her friends.
ISBN 978-1-4424-4168-2 (pbk. : alk. paper) — ISBN 978-1-4424-4169-9 (hardcover : alk. paper) — ISBN 978-1-4424-4170-5 (ebook : alk. paper)
[1. Witches—Fiction. 2. Magic—Fiction. 3. Halloween—Fiction.
4. Costume—Fiction. 5. Behavior—Fiction.] I. Burris, Priscilla, ill. II. Title.
PZ7.C83392Hwi 2012
[Fic]—dc23
2011020323

CONTENTS

Chapter 1

WiTCH'S HONOR

Witches!

Ghosts!

And one big ol' grump-a-saurus!

Heidi Heckelbeck was the only witch who didn't like Halloween. Well, to be honest, she *did* like the spooky decorations and the candy. She even liked carving pumpkins, which she was doing right now. But there was one thing that wrecked Halloween for Heidi: people who dressed up as witches.

"I don't get it," said Heidi as she scooped stringy pumpkin goop from her pumpkin. "Real witches are nothing like the witches you read about in storybooks."

"What do you mean?" asked her little brother, Henry, as he squeezed a fistful of pumpkin seeds into a mixing bowl.

"Everyone thinks that witches have warts and fly on broomsticks," said Heidi.

"Well, some do," said Mom.

"But most of them don't," Heidi said. "I think it's weird when people dress up as witches. It's like they're making fun of us—and it bugs me."

"So dress up as something else,"
said Henry. "You could be a pirate,
like me!"

"No thanks," Heidi said. "This year
I'm going to skip Halloween."

"Are you crazy?" asked Henry. "You
won't get any FREE candy!"

Oh, drat, thought Heidi. *Henry is*

right. I love candy, but I won't get any if I skip Halloween. But the idea of trick-or-treating with kids dressed as witches is worse. Halloween is off for me. Then she looked at Henry with sweet, puppy-dog eyes.

"Will you share your Halloween candy with me?" asked Heidi.

"HELLO. Did your brain just fall out?" Henry asked. "Pirates DO NOT share their booty."

"Fine," said Heidi. "I'll have leftover family candy."

Heidi turned to Mom.

"Mom, what are we giving out for Halloween?" she asked.

"Dad's Soda-Pop Tops," said Mom.

"No chocolate bars?" asked Heidi.

"Not this year," Mom said. "Dad wants to give out his new candy. He's been working on it for months. It's not even for sale yet."

Heidi loved Dad's new Soda-Pop Tops. Each candy was shaped like a bottle cap. When you put one on your tongue, it fizzed. But Heidi could get

free samples from Dad anytime. Heidi wanted those mini chocolate bars— lots of them.

"Harumph," said Heidi.

"Well, that's what happens when you skip Halloween," said Mom as she helped scrape the last of the pulp from the pumpkins.

"Do you still want to carve some jack-o'-lantern faces?" asked Mom.

"I do!" said Henry.

"What kind of face do you want?"

"I want a goofy face!" Henry said.

Then Mom looked at Heidi.

Heidi scowled. "I want a MAD face. With pointy teeth."

"You could put a pointy hat on top too," suggested Henry. "Like a mean ol' witch!"

"Watch it, bud," said Heidi, "or I'll turn you into a FROG."

Chapter 2

WEiRDO!

Heidi's class was making place mats for their Halloween party. They cut out black cats, pumpkins, and full moons from construction paper. Heidi named her cat Creepers. It had an arched back and a frizzy tail.

While working, everyone talked about dressing up for Halloween.

"I'm going to be a skeleton!" said Stanley Stonewrecker.

"I'm going to be a prima ballerina!" said Lucy Lancaster.

"I'm going to be a mad scientist!" said Bruce Bickerson.

"But that makes no sense," said Melanie Maplethorpe. "You already

ARE a mad scientist!" Melanie was famous for saying mean things. She usually picked on Heidi.

Bruce glared at Melanie. "You're just a wicked WITCH!" he said.

"That's really funny," Melanie said, "because that's exactly what I'm going to be for Halloween—a WITCH! How did you know?"

"Just a feeling," said Bruce.

"Well, JUST SO EVERYONE KNOWS,

nobody can copy me," said Melanie. "I want to be the ONLY witch in the class."

Lucy squished Heidi's foot under the desk and whispered, "She IS the only witch in the class!"

Heidi usually laughed when Lucy made a joke, but not this time.

Melanie's NOT the only witch in the class! thought Heidi. *She doesn't know the first thing about REAL witches. She's going to be a stupid storybook witch, and that's what gives real witches a bad name.*

Melanie stopped cutting out her cat and looked at Heidi. Heidi's face had turned bright red. She looked like she might explode at any second.

"What's YOUR problem, weirdo?" asked Melanie.

Heidi wanted to scream a million mean things in Melanie's face, but she felt totally tongue-tied. Heidi made her meanest face ever instead. But Melanie kept right on talking.

"So, Miss Weirdo, have you picked out a Halloween costume?"

"None of your business," said Heidi, trying to sound tough.

"Well, no need to bother," Melanie said. "Be what you are—a total NUT!"

"Melanie Maplethorpe!" said Lucy, with her hands on her hips. "If I looked up 'evil' in the dictionary, I'd find a picture of you."

"Why, thank you!" said Melanie. "That's the nicest thing anyone's said to me all day." Then she flipped her blond hair over her shoulder and began to walk away. "And by the way," she added, turning to Heidi, "as long as we're playing Dictionary, we all know the definition of 'weirdo' is Heidi."

Melanie's words made Heidi madder than a mad cat! She scrunched her fingers like the claws of a cat and swiped the air in front of her.

"Rrrear! Siss! Phtt! Phtt! Phtt!"

"Wow," said Melanie. "You really ARE a weirdo!"

"Okay, that does it!" Heidi said. "Halloween is BACK ON!"

"What's that supposed to mean?" asked Melanie.

"You'll see," said Heidi, folding her arms. Heidi didn't know what she was going to do, but she was sure about two things: She was NOT a weirdo. . . . And she had to get a costume.

CLOWNING AROUND

Heidi slammed the car door and bounced onto the backseat.

"Hey, Heidi," said Henry.

Heidi stuck out her tongue at Henry.

"What did *I* do?" Henry asked.

"You're being too cheery," said Heidi.

Mom peeked around her seat.

"Apologize to your brother," she said.

Heidi looked at Henry sitting in his booster seat. He had on his pirate costume. He had wanted to wear it all week.

"I'm WAIT-ing," said Henry.

"SOR-ry," Heidi said.

"That's more like it," said Henry.

"Merg," growled Heidi.

"What on earth is the matter?" asked Mom.

"Nothing . . . I need a dumb ol' Halloween costume!" said Heidi.

"Why didn't you say so?" asked Mom. "If you can be polite, I would be

happy to stop at the Costume Corner
on the way home."

Heidi agreed to be polite. She was
thankful Mom didn't ask any more
questions. She didn't feel like talking
about Melanie and her crummy witch
costume. Heidi began to calm down.

When they got to the store, they browsed up and down the aisles. There were wigs, devil horns, and all kinds of funny glasses.

"I found size eight costumes," said Mom.

Heidi ran to the rack. She found a policeman costume, a fireman costume, and all kinds of superhero costumes.

"These are all BOY costumes," she said.

Mom pulled a blue-and-white-checked dress from the rack.

"How about Dorothy?" Mom asked.

"No way," said Heidi. "Not after Melanie played Dorothy in the class play."

"You can wear your scary apple tree costume," suggested Henry.

"Like I would ever do THAT again," said Heidi.

Heidi had played the role of a scary apple tree in her class play, *The Wizard of Oz.* It had been *so* embarrassing.

"Here's a nice clown costume," said Mom.

She shook a clown jumpsuit in

Heidi's direction. It was red with yellow polka dots. It also had three gigantic blue pom-poms down the front. It came with a frizzy rainbow wig, huge floppy red shoes, and—worst of all—a big red nose.

Heidi made a face. "Clowns are dumb," she said.

"It's the best we can do," Mom said. "Halloween is tomorrow."

Heidi sighed. *Well, maybe it's not that bad,* she thought.

"Okay," Heidi said. "Let's get it."

As they headed for the cash register, Heidi heard a voice behind her.

"Well, if it isn't Heidi Heckelbeck . . . ,"
someone said.

Heidi whirled around. It was Melanie.

"What are YOU doing here?" asked
Heidi.

"I'm here to get a witch's nose for
my costume. I want one that's crooked
and super-ugly."

"Not all witches have ugly, crooked noses," snapped Heidi.

"REAL witches do," said Melanie.

"They do NOT," said Heidi.

"How would you know?" Melanie asked.

Heidi didn't know what to say. She couldn't exactly tell Melanie the truth about witches. And she definitely couldn't say, *Guess what, Melanie, I just happen to be a REAL witch!* And even if she did, Melanie would never believe her. She would just think Heidi was a bigger weirdo than ever. So Heidi just said, "Never mind!"

Then she turned and stomped toward the front of the store.

Melanie called out after her, "See you later, weirdo!"

Chapter 4

JACKPOT!

Heidi stepped into her clown costume. Then she stuffed her hair into the rainbow wig and walked into the kitchen. Her family had been waiting at the kitchen table.

"So funny!" said Mom.

"So colorful!" said Dad.

"So DUMB!" said Henry.

Heidi's shoulders slumped. *It IS dumb,* she thought.

"I feel like a complete doofus," she said.

Heidi ran to her room and pulled off her wig and the rest of the clown costume. Then she flopped onto her bed with a big sigh.

This is all Melanie's fault, Heidi thought. *She had no right to talk about witches. Like she knows anything! Do I ride on a broomstick? No! Do I have*

one single wart? No! And besides that,
MELANIE'S the weirdo. She dresses like
a frilly pink cupcake. Her shoes look
like ballerina slippers. And her hair
looks like a Barbie doll's.

Then Heidi got an idea. If Melanie
was going to dress up as a witch, then

Heidi would dress up as Melanie!
Heidi ran to her closet to look for an
outfit. *Oh dear,* she thought. *I don't*

own anything pink, and I have nothing with sparkles or ruffles. . . . Wait
a sec! What about the girly outfit that
Aunt Shirley gave me for my birthday?

Heidi spied a large white box on her top shelf. She stood on a chair and carried it down. Then she pulled

off the lid, and under the purple tissue paper she found a pink skirt with one, two, three layers of ruffles. Also in the box were a pink striped top and a matching pink sweater.

"Jackpot!" cried Heidi.

She held the outfit up to the mirror.

"Wow," she said. "This is SO Melanie!"

Then Heidi frowned at herself.
*Hmm . . . my short red hair is going
to be a problem,* she thought. *I need
to have long, blond Barbie doll hair.*

Maybe Henry has a wig in his costume trunk. She zoomed down the hall to Henry's room.

"Ahoy, thar!" said Henry. "Ye best beware of the crocodiles!"

Henry was standing on top of a chair. There were stuffed animals all over the floor. He jabbed the air with a plastic sword.

Heidi tiptoed through the crocodiles. Then she kneeled down to open Henry's costume trunk.

"What ye be looking for, matey?" Henry asked.

"A wig," said Heidi.

"Arr! I'm fresh out of wigs!" said Henry. "Though may I interest you in some rotten green teeth?"

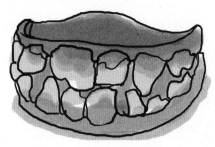

"No thanks," Heidi said. "I need a long blond wig for my Halloween costume."

"I had me a fine shipmate named Dudley," said Henry. "His mom's hair changed from short and brown to long and yellow. Maybe yours can become long and yellow too!"

Heidi dropped an armful of sashes and capes back into the trunk.

"THAT'S IT!" cried Heidi. "Thank you, Captain Kiddo!" She hugged Henry and zoomed back to her room.

"Anytime, m'lady!" said Henry.

Chapter 5

LONG AND SILKY

Goldilocks!

Rapunzel!

Smell-a-nie!

Heidi pulled her *Book of Spells* from under the bed and opened to Chapter 12: Beauty Tips. She ran her finger down the page and found the section on hair color. There were so many kinds of blond hair: Mega Blond, Dream Blond, Golden Blond, Beach Blond, and many others.

This hair seems just like Melanie's, thought Heidi. It was called Long and Silky Blond. Heidi read over the spell.

Long and Silky Blond

Is your short hair the color of a field mouse? Have you secretly always wanted to have long, flowing blond hair? Are you the kind of witch who would rather look like an angel? Then this is the spell for an all-new YOU!

Ingredients:

◯ 1 egg

✎ 3 squirts of lemon juice

◊ 2 drops of yellow food coloring

SUGAR 1 packet of sugar

Tuck your hair inside a shower cap. Place the ingredients in a plastic bowl and mix everything with a silver spoon. Hold your Witches of Westwick medallion in your left hand. Hold your right hand over the mix and chant the following words:

WITH THIS BEAUTY SALON
POTION
MY PLAN GOES INTO MOTION.
MIX THIS BREW
AND YOU WILL SEE
HOW LONG AND BLOND
MY HAIR CAN BE!

Remove the shower cap. Voilà!

This is perfect, thought Heidi. Now all I have to do is collect the ingredients. Then I can turn myself into a *Melanie look-alike!* Heidi snapped shut her *Book of Spells* and snuck down to the kitchen.

Nobody was around. *This will be a breeze!* Heidi thought. She started to collect the spell ingredients, including the bowl and spoon, in a shopping bag. *Now all I need is an egg. . . .*

Heidi opened the fridge and gently lifted an egg from the egg carton. Then she heard footsteps. *Uh-oh,* she thought. *Somebody's coming!* Heidi quickly slid the egg into the front pocket of her skirt. She set the bag down beside the fridge and froze.

Mom walked into the kitchen and almost bumped into Heidi.

"Whoa," said Mom. "What are *you* up to?"

Heidi smiled sheepishly. "Nothing."

"You look *very* guilty," Mom said.

"Just getting an apple," said Heidi. "That's all."

Mom frowned.

Then Heidi picked an apple from the fruit bowl and polished it on her shirt.

As soon as her mom turned her back, Heidi grabbed the shopping bag and dashed to her room. Then she packed her costume and the spell ingredients in her backpack. She snagged a shower

cap from the hook on the back of the
bathroom door. She wrapped the egg
in toilet paper and taped it.

*Tomorrow at school I will become
evil Melanie Maplethorpe's twin sister,*
thought Heidi. *And nobody can stop
me! Moo-hoo-haa-haa-haa!*

Chapter 6

MELANiE'S TWiN

Heidi ducked into the girls' bathroom before school started. She changed into her Melanie costume and tucked her hair in the shower cap. Then she measured her spell ingredients in the plastic bowl and mixed them with the silver spoon. She held her medallion in her left hand and held her right hand over the mix.

As Heidi chanted the spell her head began to tingle. *It's working,* she thought. She could hardly wait to see her new hairdo. She stepped in front of the mirror and removed the shower cap.

Heidi gasped. "Oh my gosh! I look just like Melanie!"

Heidi posed this way and that. She even made snooty Melanie faces in the mirror.

Wow! This is going to be the best Halloween ever! She flung her backpack over her shoulder and skipped down the hall. Then she stood in the classroom doorway with her hands on her hips—just like Melanie.

"Ahem!" said Heidi.

Bruce—who had on a frizzy white wig, green-rimmed goggles, and a lab coat—noticed Heidi and pointed.

"Heidi dressed up as MELANIE!" he said.

"That is the best costume EVER!"
Lucy said to Heidi.

Everyone in the class clapped and
laughed. Everyone except Melanie,
that is.

Melanie walked over to Heidi. "That is NOT funny," she said.

"Well, I think it's VERY funny," said Heidi. She did a little Melanie twirl and walked back to her desk and sat down. Then Heidi raised her hand.

"Yes, Heidi," said their teacher, Mrs. Welli.

Heidi pinched her nose. "Something's smelly, Mrs. Welli."

The class giggled.

"Settle down, class," said Mrs. Welli. She turned to Heidi. "That's enough."

Heidi smiled sweetly. Then she turned and made a mean face at Melanie—just like Melanie had done on Heidi's first day of school. Melanie looked away.

Later at the class party Heidi bossed everyone around—even her best friend, Lucy.

"Get me some juice!" ordered Heidi.

"Well, okay," Lucy said.

"And make it snappy!" said Heidi as she tapped her foot impatiently.

Lucy rolled her eyes and walked to the juice station.

When it was time to eat doughnuts from a string, Heidi butted in line.

"Me first!" said Heidi.

Everyone stepped aside—just like they did when Melanie wanted to be first.

During the Halloween parade on the playground, Heidi made fun of her classmates' costumes.

"Hey, Melanie!" said Heidi. "That witch outfit is a good look for you. You should wear that fake nose every day!"

Melanie looked crushed. "Why are you being so mean?" she asked.

"I'm not being mean," Heidi said. "I'm being YOU!" Then Heidi skipped away to catch up with Lucy and Bruce.

"It's so much fun being Melanie!" said Heidi. "My costume is THE BEST!"

"Uh . . . you're getting a little bit carried away," said Lucy.

"Am NOT!" snapped Heidi. "You're just jealous of my costume."

"What do you mean?" asked Lucy.

"I mean, who wants to be a dumb ballerina, anyway?" asked Heidi. "And

Bruce, Melanie's right. You already ARE a mad scientist—so that's not really much of a costume."

Lucy and Bruce stopped walking.

"You know what?" said Lucy. "Your Melanie act has gotten a little too real for me. Come on, Bruce."

"Gladly," Bruce said. "You know, I'm not sure I want to be friends with Melanie's even-more-evil twin sister."

They walked away and left Heidi all alone.

Heidi folded her arms. *What's THEIR problem?* she wondered.

Then somebody tapped Heidi on the shoulder. It was Principal Pennypacker. He had been watching Heidi from across the playground.

"We need to talk," he said.

Chapter 7

BUG SQUASHING

Heidi sat down on a bench beside Principal Pennypacker. The Halloween parade had just ended. Heidi watched the ghosts, skeletons, pumpkins, and fairies file back to their classrooms. Principal Pennypacker turned to Heidi.

"Have you ever wished you could

turn Melanie into a bug and squash her?" asked Principal Pennypacker.

Heidi gulped.

Turn Melanie into a bug? thought Heidi. *Does Principal Pennypacker know I'm a witch? But how? Or is he just trying to be funny?* Heidi looked at the principal. He wasn't smiling. Heidi decided to act like he was asking her a normal, everyday question.

"Definitely," she answered.

"I see," said the principal. "And how did it feel to be Melanie for a day?"

"It felt AMAZING," said Heidi. "It made me feel powerful!"

"I'm sure it did," said the principal. "But how do you think it made Melanie feel?"

"Who cares?" said Heidi.

"Would you like it if somebody dressed up as you?" he asked.

Heidi began to get mad. *But Melanie DID dress up as me—only she was a dumb storybook witch,* thought Heidi. *And I didn't like it ONE BIT!*

Heidi folded her arms. She knew she couldn't say that to Principal Pennypacker. So she just said, "I wouldn't like it."

"And how do you think your friends
felt when you were mean and bossy?"
asked the principal.

Hold on now! thought Heidi. *I only
PRETENDED to be Melanie. It wasn't*

for real. It was just for fun. But now that Heidi thought about it, maybe it had seemed real to her friends. They had gotten pretty mad at her. Bruce had even said he didn't want to be friends with her.

"Okay," Heidi said. "Maybe I got a little carried away."

Principal Pennypacker nodded thoughtfully. "Maybe just a little."

Then the bell rang and everyone began to pour back onto the playground. Principal Pennypacker patted Heidi on the shoulder and smiled. "Happy Halloween," he said.

"Thanks," said Heidi.

Heidi got her backpack from her classroom and headed for pickup. Mom and Henry were waiting for her in the car.

Chapter 8

BEASTLY FEELINGS

"You're in BIG trouble," said Henry as Heidi got into the car.

Heidi looked at her mom.

"Henry said you were not very nice at school today," said Mom.

Heidi sighed. "I decided to be Melanie for Halloween," she said. "But

I guess I went a teeny bit overboard."

"I'll say," Henry said. "She wouldn't even say hi to me in the hallway!"

"I'm sorry," said Heidi. "I was a total creep."

"You can say THAT again," said Henry. "But you know what? Your Melanie act was SO AMAZING. You were JUST like her. You should go to Hollywood!"

"Thanks, bud."

"Come on," said Mom. "Is Melanie really all that bad?"

"Sometimes," said Heidi.

"Well, believe it or not, she has feelings too," said Mom.

"You could've fooled me."

"Me too," said Henry.

"Trust me," Mom said. "Melanie has feelings."

"Beastly feelings," said Heidi.

"Beastly or not—they're still feelings."

They all laughed.

"Now, about your hair, young lady . . ."

Heidi pretended that she didn't know what her Mom was talking

about. "Huh? What about it?"

Mom gave Heidi a knowing look.

"You know how I feel about you using your witching skills," said Mom.

"I know—I'm sorry," Heidi said. "But may I *please* keep my long blond hair for Halloween?"

Mom sighed. "I'll let you stay blond
for Halloween . . . on one condition."

Heidi braced herself.

"You need to call your friends—
including Melanie—and apologize as
soon as we get home," said Mom.

"Deal," said Heidi.

Chapter 9

GOOD-BYE, MELANIE!

Heidi called Lucy and Bruce to say she was sorry, but they weren't home. Neither was Melanie. *Oh, drat,* thought Heidi. *They will never speak to me again. I wish I hadn't been such a stinker!* Heidi twirled her hair around her finger and stared at the wall.

Just then Mom entered the kitchen with a box full of Halloween decorations. "What's wrong, sweetie?" she asked.

"I can't find anyone to trick-or-treat with me," said Heidi.

"I'm sorry to hear that," said Mom as she sorted through some candles and plastic skeletons. "But if you like,

you could trick-or-treat with Henry
and Dudley."

"Do you think they'd let me?" asked
Heidi.

"Of course," said Mom. "As long as
you leave Melanie behind."

"Trust me," Heidi said. "I'm DONE being Melanie. I'm going to turn my Melanie costume into something else."

"I like the sound of that," said Mom.

Heidi thought about what else she could be with her long, blond hair. She finally decided she would be a princess. Heidi didn't like princesses, but she didn't have much time. *Just for tonight,* she thought.

Heidi soon got to work. She cut a crown from a piece of poster board and covered it with tinfoil. Then she stapled the ends together. Heidi decorated the crown with gemstone

stickers. Finally she placed it on her head and looked in the mirror.

"Good-bye, Melanie's evil twin sister," she said to herself. "Hello, Princess Heidi."

Heidi felt better already. She helped

Mom put candles in the pumpkins, and she hung a plastic skeleton on the front door. Then Heidi and Dad put an alien dummy with flickering green lights in Henry's window. Trick-or-treaters would see the alien as they came up the front walk.

"HEL-LO, EARTHLINGS!" said Heidi, pretending to be an alien.

Henry looked a little worried. "Do I have to sleep in the room with the alien?" he asked.

"But you ARE an alien," said Heidi. "You should feel right at home."

"Very funny," said Henry, but he could tell his sister was joking.

Dad promised to take down the alien before Henry went to bed. Then Dad piled his Soda-Pop Top candies into an orange plastic bowl by the front door. He couldn't wait to see how the trick-or-treaters would like them.

When everyone was ready, Dad set up the camera and took a Halloween family picture.

"Yo ho ho! It's time to go!" shouted Henry. Henry had a pillowcase for his pirate booty in one hand and his sword in the other.

"Her royal highness is ready too!" said Heidi.

When Dudley—who was dressed as a mummy—arrived, they set out trick-or-treating. Dudley's mom and Heidi's mom followed close behind, while Heidi's dad stayed home to give out candy. The kids ran from house to house.

This is kind of fun, thought Heidi. *But it would be even more fun if I was with my own friends. Will they ever like me again?*

Chapter 10

TRICK OR TREAT!

It was bound to happen and, of course, it did. Heidi bumped into Lucy and Bruce on the sidewalk.

"Hi," Heidi said, hoping her friends would say hi back.

But they didn't.

Instead, Lucy and Bruce acted as if

they couldn't even see her.

"Did somebody say something?" asked Lucy.

"I didn't hear anything," Bruce said.

"Oh, it must have been NOBODY," said Lucy.

And they kept on walking.

Heidi's shoulders slumped. The candy in her pillowcase felt heavy, which was usually a good thing. But right then it felt too heavy. She wanted to drop it and run all the way home.

Heidi decided to skip the next house, and instead she waited for Henry and Dudley on the sidewalk. As she waited, two trick-or-treaters ran down the front walk toward her. One was dressed as a witch and the other was dressed as a skeleton. They stopped when they saw Heidi.

"Oh no!" said the witch. "It's HER!"

Heidi recognized the witch too.

"Wait," said Heidi. "I have something to say."

"Like what?" asked the witch.

"Like I'm sorry for dressing up as you," said Heidi. "It was mean."

"Then why are you still dressed as

me?" asked the witch, who was really Melanie.

"I'm not," said Heidi. "Now I'm a princess. See my crown?"

Melanie looked closely at Heidi's tinfoil crown. Then something strange happened. The ends of Melanie's mouth turned up just a tiny bit. *Is that a smile?* wondered Heidi. Melanie

had never smiled at her before. Heidi
smiled back.

"Whoa," said the skeleton, who was
actually Stanley. "Did you two just get
along?"

"I think maybe they did," Lucy said,
who had come back across the street
with Bruce.

Heidi spun around.

"We decided to come back," said Lucy.

"We felt bad about being mean back there," Bruce said.

"That's okay," said Heidi. "I totally deserved it."

"You can say THAT again!" said Lucy.

"I'm sorry," said Heidi. "I REALLY am."

Lucy looked at Bruce. "Should we forgive her?" she asked.

"I suppose so," said Bruce.

"Thanks," said Heidi. "I never knew how much my friends meant to me until I almost lost them."

Then Stanley had a great idea. "Do you guys want to trick-or-treat with us?" he asked.

"Really?" questioned Heidi.

"No, NOT really," said Melanie. "I don't trick-or-treat with weirdos." Melanie stuck her nose in the air and began to walk away. "Come on, Stanley," she called over her shoulder.

Stanley hurried after Melanie.

"Well, it looks like things are back to normal," said Lucy.

"Sure does," Bruce said.

"WHATEVER," said Heidi. "Come on. . . . Let's get some CANDY!"

And they all raced to the next house and shouted, "TRICK OR TREAT!"

Lucky Lucy, thought Heidi. *She's getting so much attention for her new glasses.* Heidi had to admit, Lucy's glasses were really, really cool.

Mrs. Welli clapped her hands as she walked into the classroom.

An excerpt from *Heidi Heckelbeck Gets Glasses*

"Please take your seats, boys and girls!"

Everyone scrambled to their desks.

Mrs. Welli noticed Lucy's glasses right away.

"So stylish, Lucy," said Mrs. Welli. "And now you'll be able to see the chalkboard."

"Thanks," said Lucy with a smile.

All day everyone made a big deal about Lucy's glasses.

During English, Mrs. Welli read from a book of poems. Then she asked everyone to write their own. At the end of class Mrs. Welli asked Lucy to read hers out loud. Heidi knew why

Lucy got picked. It was because of her new glasses.

In art, Lucy got the same kind of attention. Mr. Doodlebee even drew a picture of Lucy with her glasses and hung it on the bulletin board.

I wish Mr. Doodlebee would draw a picture of me, thought Heidi. *The problem is, I don't stand out. I need a new look. . . .*

Heidi smiled to herself. *Aha! I know just how to get one.*